The Mermaid, the Prince and the Happy Ever After

Timothy Knapman

Illustrated by Adria Meserve

PUFFIN

Beachfront Castle had sprung a leak.

To be precise, Beachfront Castle had sprung lots of leaks. But the King was too poor to make repairs. He was so poor that his crown was made out of cardboard. So poor he had to get his dragon, Wilberforce, to stretch out his wings to plug the leaks.

And still it kept on raining.

"It's no good," said the King. "Pretty soon, it won't be Beachfront Castle any more, it'll be Beachfront Swimming Pool!"

"There's only one thing for it," cried the King to his son, Prince Bernard. "You'll have to marry a nice rich princess! Then we can afford to have the castle repaired!

There are plenty of princesses to choose from. Here, I've made you a list."

There was
Princess *Kip Shtum*.
But she was as quiet as a mouse.

Princess
Donna Undblitzen.
But she was as
loud as thunder.

And there was
Princess
Arabella Shazam.
But she had magic powers
and Bernard didn't fancy
being turned into a toad.

"But I won't live **happily ever after** if I marry any of them!" said Bernard, who took being a prince very seriously. He knew that living

"happily ever after"

was an important part of his job.

Just thinking about princesses made his head hurt.

Down,
down,
down
he
dived
into
the
deep
blue
sea.

So Prince Bernard put
on his chainmail trunks
and his rubber crown
and went for a swim
to clear his head.

When
suddenly,
from far away, he saw something
flash
and
glitter.

As he swam closer, he found himself looking at
the most beautiful girl he had ever seen.
She had hair as gold as goldfish.
And a smile like the sun shining on surf.

"My name's Coral.
What's yours?" she said.

Her words floated
towards Bernard
in little air bubbles.
As the bubbles
popped
against his ear,
they tickled
like
kisses.

Suddenly Bernard's head
didn't hurt any more and
he didn't stop smiling
all the way home.

"A prince can't live happily ever after
with a MERMAID!" cried the King,
when Bernard said he wanted to marry Coral.
"She'll be covered in barnacles!
She'll invite sharks round for TEA!
Hang on a minute,
is
she
rich?"

"She hasn't got two pilchards to rub together," said Bernard happily.

The King sighed. "You don't LOVE her, do you?"

Bernard went bright red.

"Oh well," said the King. "Wilberforce does love a wedding."

The King was up all night making wedding decorations from old newspapers. And Wilberforce just about managed a rather smoky firework display.

The guests shouted,

"HOORAY! Long live Prince Bernard!"

And then whispered,
"Why is he marrying a fish tank?"

Of course, the answer was that as mermaids can only breathe underwater, Coral had to live in an enormous fish tank.

And even though it was the biggest fish tank in the kingdom,
Coral was used to swimming in the wide, wide ocean.
She so missed the sea.

As the days passed, Bernard noticed the
sadness in Coral's eyes. "We'll never live
happily ever after
like this!" he said.

So, very late one night,
he wheeled Coral's fish tank
down to the beach and
tipped her back into the sea.

Then
 he
  jumped
   in
    after
     her.

Although Bernard and Coral didn't have
two pilchards to rub together,
they could have lived happily ever after
in her little shell house at the bottom of the sea,
if it hadn't been
for
one
thing . . .

. . . princes can only breathe above water.

So Bernard had to swim back up to the surface every time he needed air. And whenever he did, he gazed longingly at Beachfront Castle.

"We'll never live happily ever after like this!" said Coral.
"You're right," said Bernard sadly.

Coral was heartbroken.
Whatever happened to True Love?
How could they ever be together?

But then Bernard had an idea . . .

and

off

he

swam.

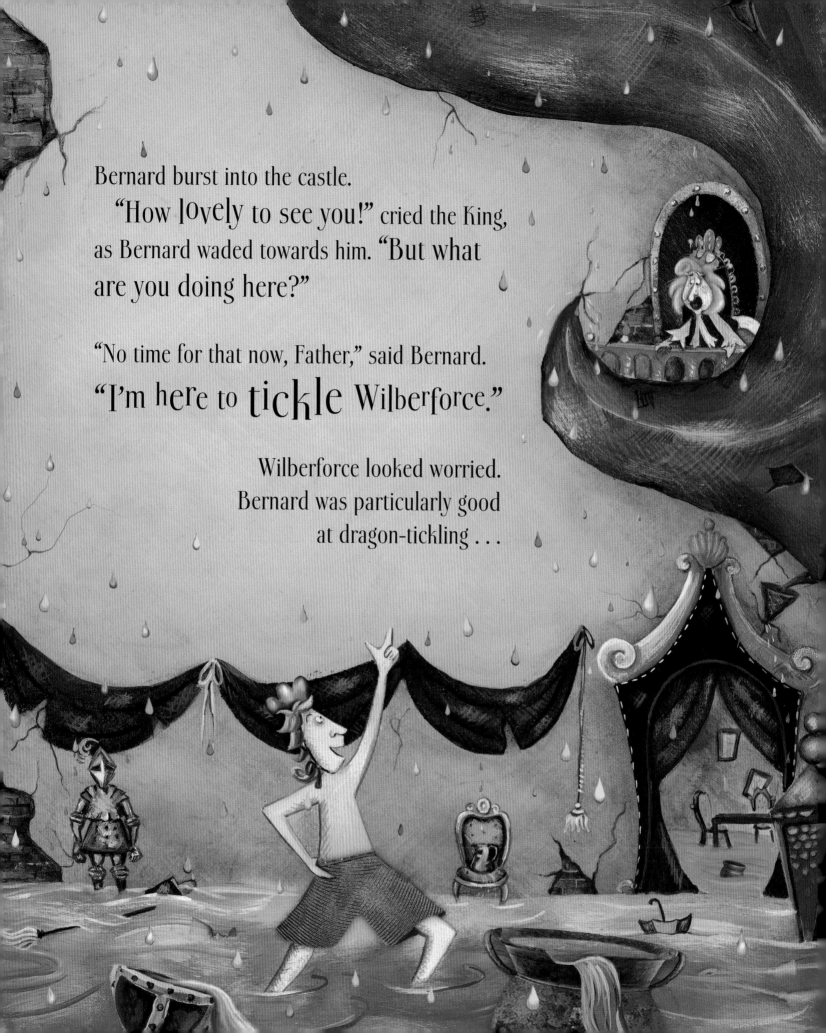

Bernard burst into the castle.

"How lovely to see you!" cried the King, as Bernard waded towards him. "But what are you doing here?"

"No time for that now, Father," said Bernard. "I'm here to tickle Wilberforce."

Wilberforce looked worried. Bernard was particularly good at dragon-tickling . . .

... and Wilberforce was a particularly ticklish dragon.

He giggled ...

... and giggled.

Until one by one ...

"Exactly!" replied Bernard. Then all at once the water came WHOOSHING and SWOOSHING in. Suddenly the castle was alive with fountains and waterfalls!

As the waters rose,
Coral swam in from the sea
and straight into Bernard's arms.
"Together at last!" they cried.
"Now we'll never be parted again!"

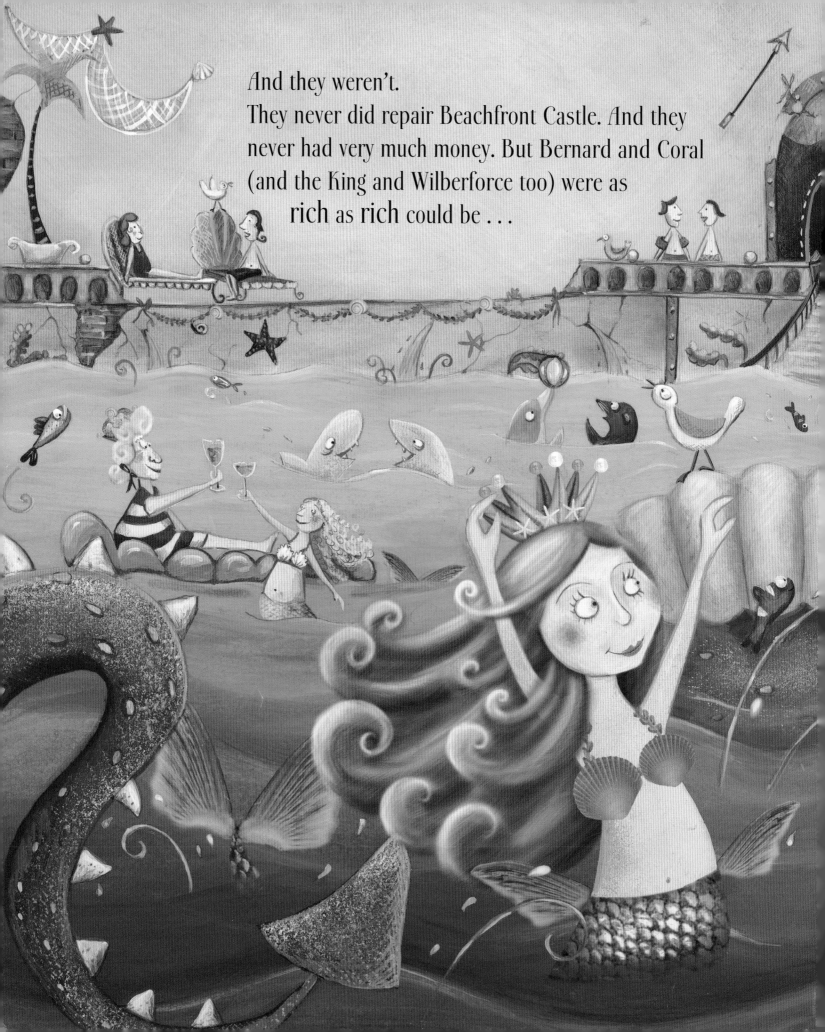

And they weren't.
They never did repair Beachfront Castle. And they
never had very much money. But Bernard and Coral
(and the King and Wilberforce too) were as
rich as rich could be . . .

because at last they could live
happily ever after.

The End

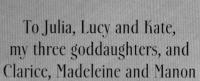

To Julia, Lucy and Kate,
my three goddaughters, and
Clarice, Madeleine and Manon
with love – T.K.

For Ian, my very own
Prince Bernard, with love – A.M.

PUFFIN BOOKS
Published by the Penguin Group:
London, New York, Australia, Canada,
India, Ireland, New Zealand and South Africa
Penguin Books Ltd, Registered Offices:
80 Strand, London WC2R 0RL, England

penguin.com

First published in Puffin Books 2007
3 5 7 9 10 8 6 4 2
Text copyright © Timothy Knapman, 2007
Illustrations copyright © Adria Meserve, 2007
Made and printed in China
ISBN: 978-0-140-56999-5